ARROW BOOK OF
Ghost Stories

Edited by
NORA KRAMER

Illustrated by George Wilde

SCHOLASTIC BOOK SERVICES
New York Toronto London Auckland Sydney Tokyo

D1021867

CONTENTS

To

My Own Ghost-Story Enthusiasts—

Dinnie and Joan

The King o' the Cats

BY JOSEPH JACOBS

ONE WINTER'S EVENING the Sexton's wife was sitting by the fireside with her big black cat, Old Tom, on the other side, both half asleep and wait-

1

ing for the master to come home. They waited and they waited, but still he didn't come, till at last he came rushing in, calling out, "Who's Tommy Tildrum?" in such a wild way that both his wife and the cat stared at him to know what was the matter.

"Why, what's the matter?" said his wife, "and why do you want to know who Tommy Tildrum is?"

"Oh, I've had such an adventure. I was digging away at old Mr. Fordyce's grave when I suppose I must have fallen asleep, and only woke up by hearing a cat's *miaou*."

"*Miaou!*" said Old Tom in answer.

"Yes, just like that! So I looked over the edge of the grave, and what do you think I saw?"

"Now, how can I tell?" said the Sexton's wife.

"Why, nine black cats all like our friend Old Tom here, all with a white spot on their chests. And what do you think they were carrying? Why, a small coffin covered with a black velvet pall, and on the pall was a small coronet all of gold, and at every third step they took they cried all together, '*Miaou—!*'"

2

"*Miaou!*" said Old Tom again.

"Yes, just like that!" said the Sexton; "and as they came nearer and nearer to me I could see them more distinctly, because their eyes shone with a sort of green light. Well, they all came towards me, eight of them carrying the coffin, and the biggest cat of all walking in front for all the world like—but look at Old Tom, how he's looking at me. You'd think he knew all I was saying."

"Go on, go on," said his wife, "never mind Old Tom."

"Well, as I was a-saying, they came towards me slowly and solemnly, and at every third step crying all together, '*Miaou—*'"

"*Miaou!*" said Old Tom again.

"Yes, just like that, till they came and stood right opposite Mr. Fordyce's grave, where I was, when they all stood still and looked straight at me. I did feel queer, that I did! But look at Old Tom; he's looking at me just like they did."

"Go on, go on," said his wife, "never mind Old Tom."

"Where was I? Oh, they all stood still looking at me, when the one that wasn't carrying the

3

coffin came forward and, staring straight at me, said to me, with a squeaky voice, 'Tell Tom Tildrum that Tim Toldrum's dead,' and that's why I asked you if you know who Tom Tildrum was, for how can I tell Tom Tildrum Tim Toldrum's dead if I don't know who Tom Tildrum is?"

"Look at Old Tom, look at Old Tom!" screamed his wife.

And well he might look, for Old Tom was swelling and Old Tom was staring, and at last Old Tom shrieked out, "What—Old Tim dead! Then I'm the King o' the Cats!" and rushed up the chimney and was never more seen.

Jimmy Takes Vanishing Lessons

BY WALTER R. BROOKS

T HE SCHOOL BUS picked up Jimmy Crandall every
morning at the side road that led up to his aunt's

house, and every afternoon it dropped him there again. And so twice a day, on the bus, he passed the entrance to the mysterious road.

It wasn't much of a road any more. It was choked with weeds and blackberry bushes, and the woods on both sides pressed in so closely that the branches met overhead, and it was dark and gloomy even on bright days. The bus driver once pointed it out.

"Folks that go in there after dark," he said, "well, they usually don't ever come out again. There's a haunted house about a quarter of a mile down that road." He paused. "But you ought to know about that, Jimmy. It was your grandfather's house."

Jimmy knew about it, and he knew that it now belonged to his Aunt Mary. But Jimmy's aunt would never talk to him about the house. She said the stories about it were silly nonsense and there were no such things as ghosts. If all the villagers weren't a lot of superstitious idiots, she would be able to rent the house, and then she would have enough money to buy Jimmy some decent clothes and take him to the movies.

Jimmy thought it was all very well to say that

there were no such things as ghosts, but how about the people who had tried to live there? Aunt Mary had rented the house three times, but every family had moved out within a week. They said the things that went on there were just too queer. So nobody would live in it any more.

Jimmy thought about the house a lot. If he could only prove that there wasn't a ghost. . . . And one Saturday when his aunt was in the village, Jimmy took the key to the haunted house from its hook on the kitchen door, and started out.

It had seemed like a fine idea when he had first thought of it—to find out for himself. Even in the silence and damp gloom of the old road it still seemed pretty good. Nothing to be scared of, he told himself. Ghosts aren't around in the daytime. But when he came out in the clearing and looked at those blank, dusty windows, he wasn't so sure.

"Oh, come on!" he told himself. And he squared his shoulders and waded through the long grass to the porch.

Then he stopped again. His feet did not seem to want to go up the steps. It took him nearly five minutes to persuade them to move. But when at

7

last they did, they marched right up and across the porch to the front door, and Jimmy set his teeth hard and put the key in the keyhole. It turned with a squeak. He pushed the door open and went in.

That was probably the bravest thing that Jimmy had ever done. He was in a long dark hall with closed doors on both sides, and on the right there were stairs going up. He had left the door open behind him, and the light from it showed him that, except for the hatrack and table and chairs, the hall was empty. And then as he stood there, listening to the bumping of his heart, gradually the light faded, the hall grew darker and darker —as if something huge had come up on the porch behind him and stood there, blocking the doorway. He swung round quickly, but there was nothing there.

He drew a deep breath. It must have been just a cloud passing across the sun. But then the door, all by itself, began to swing shut. And before he could stop it, it closed with a bang. And it was then, as he was pulling frantically at the handle to get out, that Jimmy saw the ghost.

It behaved just as you would expect a ghost to behave. It was a tall, dim, white figure, and it came gliding slowly down the stairs towards him. Jimmy gave a yell, yanked the door open, and tore down the steps.

He didn't stop until he was well down the road. Then he had to get his breath. He sat down on a log. "Boy!" he said. "I've seen a ghost! Golly, was that awful!" Then after a minute, he thought, "What was so awful about it? He was trying to scare me, like that smart aleck who was always jumping out from behind things. Pretty silly business for a grown-up ghost to be doing."

It always makes you mad when someone deliberately tries to scare you. And as Jimmy got over his fright, he began to get angry. And pretty soon he got up and started back. "I must get that key, anyway," he thought, for he had left it in the door.

This time he approached very quietly. He thought he'd just lock the door and go home. But as he tiptoed up the steps he saw it was still open; and as he reached out cautiously for the key, he heard a faint sound. He drew back and peeked

9

around the doorjamb, and there was the ghost.

The ghost was going back upstairs, but he wasn't gliding now, he was doing a sort of dance, and every other step he would bend double and shake with laughter. His thin cackle was the sound Jimmy had heard. Evidently he was enjoying the joke he had played.

That made Jimmy madder than ever. He stuck his head farther around the doorjamb and yelled "Boo!" at the top of his lungs. The ghost gave a thin shriek and leaped two feet in the air, then collapsed on the stairs.

As soon as Jimmy saw he could scare the ghost even worse than the ghost could scare him, he wasn't afraid any more, and he came right into the hall. The ghost was hanging on the banisters and panting. "Oh, my goodness!" he gasped. "Oh, my gracious! Boy, you can't *do* that to me!"

"I did it, didn't I?" said Jimmy. "Now we're even."

"Nothing of the kind," said the ghost crossly. "You seem pretty stupid, even for a boy. Ghosts are supposed to scare people. People aren't supposed to scare ghosts." He got up slowly and glided

10

down and sat on the bottom step. "But look here, boy; this could be pretty serious for me if people got to know about it."

"You mean you don't want me to tell anybody about it?" Jimmy asked.

"Suppose we make a deal," the ghost said. "You keep still about this, and in return I'll—well, let's see; how would you like to know how to vanish?"

"Oh, that would be swell!" Jimmy exclaimed. "But—can you vanish?"

"Sure," said the ghost, and he did. All at once he just wasn't there. Jimmy was alone in the hall.

But his voice went right on. "It would be pretty handy, wouldn't it?" he said persuasively. "You could get into the movies free whenever you wanted to, and if your aunt called you to do something—when you were in the yard, say—well, she wouldn't be able to find you."

"I don't mind helping Aunt Mary," Jimmy said.

"H'm. High-minded, eh?" said the ghost. "Well, then—"

"I wish you'd please reappear," Jimmy interrupted. "It makes me feel funny to talk to somebody who isn't there."

"Sorry, I forgot," said the ghost, and there he was again, sitting on the bottom step. Jimmy could see the step, dimly, right through him. "Good trick, eh? Well, if you don't like vanishing, maybe I could teach you to seep through keyholes. Like this." He floated over to the door and went right through the keyhole, the way water goes down the drain. Then he came back the same way.

"That's useful, too," he said. "Getting into locked rooms and so on. You can go anywhere the wind can."

"No," said Jimmy. "There's only one thing you can do to get me to promise not to tell about scaring you. Go live somewhere else. There's Miller's, up the road. Nobody lives there any more."

"That old shack!" said the ghost, with a nasty laugh. "Doors and windows half off, roof leaky— no thanks! What do you think it's like in a storm, windows banging, rain dripping on you—I guess not! Peace and quiet, that's really what a ghost wants out of life."

"Well, I don't think it's very fair," Jimmy said, "for you to live in a house that doesn't belong to you and keep my aunt from renting it."

13

"Pooh!" said the ghost. "I'm not stopping her from renting it. I don't take up any room, and it's not my fault if people get scared and leave."

"It certainly is!" Jimmy said angrily. "You don't play fair and I'm not going to make any bargain with you. I'm going to tell everybody how I scared you."

"Oh, you mustn't do that!" The ghost seemed quite disturbed and he vanished and reappeared rapidly several times. "If that got out, every ghost in the country would be in terrible trouble."

So they argued about it. The ghost said if Jimmy wanted money he could learn to vanish; then he could join a circus and get a big salary. Jimmy said he didn't want to be in a circus; he wanted to go to college and learn to be a doctor. He was very firm. And the ghost began to cry. "But this is my *home*, boy," he said. "Thirty years I've lived here and no trouble to anybody, and now you want to throw me out into the cold world! And for what? A little money! That's pretty heartless." And he sobbed, trying to make Jimmy feel cruel.

Jimmy didn't feel cruel at all, for the ghost had

14

certainly driven plenty of other people out into
the cold world. But he didn't really think it would
do much good for him to tell anybody that he
had scared the ghost. Nobody would believe him,
and how could he prove it? So after a minute he
said, "Well, all right. You teach me to vanish and
I won't tell." They settled it that way.

Jimmy didn't say anything to his aunt about
what he'd done. But every Saturday he went to
the haunted house for his vanishing lesson. It is
really quite easy when you know how, and in a
couple of weeks he could flicker, and in six weeks
the ghost gave him an examination and he got a
B plus, which is very good for a human. So he
thanked the ghost and shook hands with him and
said, "Well, good-by now. You'll hear from me."

"What do you mean by that?" said the ghost
suspiciously. But Jimmy just laughed and ran off
home.

That night at supper Jimmy's aunt said, "Well,
what have you been doing today?"

"I've been learning to vanish."

His aunt smiled and said, "That must be fun."

15

"Honestly," said Jimmy. "The ghost up at grandfather's house taught me."

"I don't think that's very funny," said his aunt. "And will you please not—why, where are you?" she demanded, for he had vanished.

"Here, Aunt Mary," he said as he reappeared.

"Merciful heavens!" she exclaimed, and she pushed back her chair and rubbed her eyes hard. Then she looked at him again.

Well, it took a lot of explaining and he had to do it twice more before he could persuade her that he really could vanish. She was pretty upset. But at last she calmed down and they had a long talk. Jimmy kept his word and didn't tell her that he had scared the ghost, but he said he had a plan, and at last, though very reluctantly, she agreed to help him.

So the next day she went up to the old house and started to work. She opened the windows and swept and dusted and aired the bedding, and made as much noise as possible. This disturbed the ghost, and pretty soon he came floating into the room where she was sweeping. She was scared all right. She gave a yell and threw the broom at him. As the broom went right through him and he came nearer, waving his arms and groaning, she shrank back.

And Jimmy, who had been standing there invisible all the time, suddenly appeared and jumped at the ghost with a "Boo!" And the ghost fell over in a dead faint.

As soon as Jimmy's aunt saw that, she wasn't frightened any more. She found some smelling salts and held them under the ghost's nose, and when he came to she tried to help him into a chair. Of course, she couldn't help him much because her hands went right through him. But at last he sat up and said reproachfully to Jimmy, "You broke your word!"

"I promised not to tell about scaring you," said the boy, "but I didn't promise not to scare you again."

And his aunt said, "You really are a ghost, aren't you? I thought you were just stories people made up. Well, excuse me, but I must get on with my work." And she began sweeping and banging around with her broom harder than ever.

The ghost put his hands to his head. "All this

17

noise," he said. "Couldn't you work more quietly, ma'am?"

"Whose house is this, anyway?" she demanded. "If you don't like it, why don't you move out?"

The ghost sneezed violently several times. "Excuse me," he said. "You're raising so much dust. Where's that boy?" he asked suddenly. For Jimmy had vanished again.

"I'm sure I don't know," she replied. "Probably getting ready to scare you again."

"You ought to have better control of him," said the ghost severely. "If he was my boy, I'd take a hairbrush to him."

"You have my permission," she said, and she reached right through the ghost and pulled the chair cushion out from under him and began banging the dust out of it. "What's more," she went on, as he got up and glided wearily to another chair, "Jimmy and I are going to sleep here nights from now on, and I don't think it would be very smart of you to try any tricks."

"Ha, ha," said the ghost nastily. "He who laughs last—"

"Ha, ha, yourself," said Jimmy's voice from close behind him. "And that's me, laughing last."

The ghost muttered and vanished.

Jimmy's aunt put cotton in her ears and slept that night in the best bedroom with the light lit. The ghost screamed for a while down in the cellar, but nothing happened, so he came upstairs. He thought he would appear to her as two glaring, fiery eyes, which was one of his best tricks, but first he wanted to be sure where Jimmy was. But he couldn't find him. He hunted all over the house, and though he was invisible himself, he got more and more nervous. He kept imagining that at any moment Jimmy might jump out at him from some dark corner and scare him into fits. Finally he got so jittery that he went back to the cellar and hid in the coalbin all night.

The following days were just as bad for the ghost. Several times he tried to scare Jimmy's aunt while she was working, but she didn't scare worth a cent, and twice Jimmy managed to sneak up on him and appear suddenly with a loud yell, frightening him dreadfully. He was, I suppose, rather timid even for a ghost. He began to look quite haggard. He had several long arguments with Jimmy's aunt, in which he wept and appealed to her sympathy, but she was firm. If he wanted to live there he would have to pay rent, just like anybody else. There was the abandoned Miller farm two miles up the road. Why didn't he move there?

When the house was all in apple-pie order, Jimmy's aunt went down to the village to see a Mr. and Mrs. Whistler, who were living at the hotel because they couldn't find a house to move into. She told them about the old house, but they said, "No, thank you. We've heard about that house. It's haunted. I'll bet," they said, "*you* wouldn't dare spend a night there."

She told them that she had spent the last week there, but they evidently didn't believe her. So she said, "You know my nephew, Jimmy. He's twelve years old. I am so sure that the house is not haunted that, if you want to rent it, I will let Jimmy stay there with you every night until you are sure everything is all right."

"Ha!" said Mr. Whistler. "The boy won't do it. He's got more sense."

So they sent for Jimmy. "Why, I've spent the last week there," he said. "Sure. I'd just as soon." But the Whistlers still refused.

So Jimmy's aunt went around and told a lot of the village people about their talk, and everybody made so much fun of the Whistlers for being afraid, when a twelve-year-old boy wasn't, that they were ashamed, and said they would rent it. So they moved in.

Jimmy stayed there for a week, but he saw nothing of the ghost. And then one day one of the boys in his grade told him that somebody had seen a ghost up at the Miller farm. So Jimmy knew the ghost had taken his aunt's advice.

A day or two later he walked up to the Miller farm. There was no front door and he walked right in. There was some groaning and thumping upstairs, and then after a minute the ghost came floating down.

"Oh, it's you!" he said. "Goodness sakes, boy, can't you leave me in peace?"

Jimmy said he'd just come up to see how he was getting along.

"Getting along fine," said the ghost. "From my

21

point of view it's a very desirable property. Peaceful. Quiet. Nobody playing silly tricks."

"Well," said Jimmy, "I won't bother you if you don't bother the Whistlers. But if you come back there—"

"Don't worry," said the ghost.

So with the rent money, Jimmy and his aunt had a much easier life. They went to the movies sometimes twice a week, and Jimmy had all new clothes, and on Thanksgiving, for the first time in his life, Jimmy had a turkey.

Once a week he would go up to the Miller farm to see the ghost and they got to be very good friends. The ghost even came down to the Thanksgiving dinner, though of course he couldn't eat much. He seemed to enjoy the warmth of the house and he was in very good humor. He taught Jimmy several more tricks. The best one was how to glare with fiery eyes, which was useful later on when Jimmy became a doctor and had to look down people's throats to see if their tonsils ought to come out. He was really a pretty good fellow as ghosts go, and Jimmy's aunt got quite fond of him herself.

When the real winter weather began, she even used to worry about him a lot, because, of course, there was no heat in the Miller place and the doors and windows didn't amount to much and there was hardly any roof. The ghost tried to explain to her that the heat and cold didn't bother ghosts at all.

"Maybe not," she said, "but just the same, it can't be very pleasant." And when he accepted their invitation for Christmas dinner she knitted some red woolen slippers, and he was so pleased that he broke down and cried. And that made Jimmy's aunt so happy, *she* broke down and cried.

Jimmy didn't cry, but he said, "Aunt Mary, don't you think it would be nice if the ghost came down and lived with us this winter?"

"I would feel very much better about him if he did," she said.

So he stayed with them that winter, and then he just stayed on, and it must have been a peaceful place for the last I heard he was still there.

The Woodman and the Goblins

BY J. B. ESENWEIN and MARIETTA STOCKARD

THERE ONCE WAS a Woodman who lived in the heart of a thick woods. He built his own house, lived in it all by himself, did his own cooking, mended his own clothes, and managed things somehow.

One afternoon he suddenly saw that his axe was quite worn out. A new axe he must have for the next day's work. He must go to the far-off village to buy a new one. He washed his face, combed his gray hair, stuck a pin through his leather clothes where some buttons were off, and set out for the village miles and miles away.

When the people saw his fat, stumpy little fig-ure coming down the street, they came out to talk to him, for he was a kind old fellow and they all liked him. He was glad to have someone to talk to, so he stayed quite late in the village. The sun was going down by the time he put his new axe across his shoulder and started for home.

"Be careful as you walk through the woods tonight," his friends warned, "you know it is Hal-loween and the witches and goblins will be out."

"If I get home before midnight, I will be safe," he thought, but he hurried faster through the woods.

Now the old Woodman would have told you that

he could find his way home with his eyes shut, but suddenly, to his great surprise, he saw that the road looked very strange. He was lost! As he went forward, the woods became thicker and thicker. The trees were so close together he could hardly squeeze through. But he walked on, jumping at every sound, for it was very dark indeed, and he could not help thinking of witches, goblins, and ghosts.

At last he came to a huge beech tree, and as he peered about trying to find a path, he saw six big eggs lying in a hollow place between the roots of the tree.

"Such thumping big eggs," he marveled. "If I can raise some hens to lay such eggs, I'll never again have far to look for breakfast."

No sooner had he picked up the eggs than the path that had been hidden by the dense trees came into view. The old Woodman carried the eggs carefully, walking very slowly so as not to stumble with his treasure.

When he got home he began to look about for some way to hatch the eggs. At last he thought of a piece of red flannel he had bought to make himself some winter shirts. He cut it up, wrapped it around each egg, and then placed them around the fire.

Night and day, for three weeks he kept the fire going. Night and day, for three weeks he turned and watched the eggs. It was a tedious job, but, of course, if one wants something one must work for it, and the Woodman wanted those big hens.

At last the eggs showed signs of life. They moved a little—just a teeny, tiny bit. First one egg began to chip. Then another. And another. One of the cracks opened, and out came—not a chicken's head as he had expected, but a little purply-black, squirmy fist.

There was a crackling and a squealing and a squirming. Out of one egg popped a head; out of another popped a foot. And soon six little bodies had wriggled out of the six eggs. *Six Gobblins!*

The Woodman stood staring at the six queer creatures sprawling and tumbling over each other on the floor. He did not know what to say, or think, or do. He could only scratch his head and stare.

He thought the poor things looked cold, so he

took the pieces of flannel that had been wrapped around the eggs, and snipped a round hole in each piece. Then he slipped the pieces over the little shivering bodies.

How was he to feed them? He brought some pans of milk, but the Goblins did not know how to drink. At last he thought of a way. He dipped some of the flannel into the milk, and put it into their gaping little mouths. After awhile he taught them to drink through a straw. Then they ate and ate and ate as if they did not know how to stop.

Of course that made them sick, and there was more trouble for the poor man. He had never been so busy in all his life. Sometimes he was so tired that he thought of running away and leaving the Goblins. But he was too kind to do that, for if they were left alone they would surely freeze and starve.

"Perhaps if I take care of them now, they will help me when they are older," he thought. "They could run errands, cook the food, chop the wood, and go to the spring for the drinking water."

But as they grew older, instead of helping him

the Goblins hindered him. They were always playing pranks. They pulled the poor cat's tail, hid
the Woodman's glasses—in fact, they were just as
bad as bad could be.

But bad as they were all day long, when the
candles were lit in the evening, they became
strangely quiet.

No matter what they were doing, the moment
they saw the flickering candles, they stopped and
gathered around the glow. They leaned their el-
bows on the table, propped their chins in their
hands, and stared at the candles, their eyes growing round as the letter O. They did not wink,
they did not blink.

One night when the Goblins were gathered
around the table, staring at the light, an idea came
to the Woodman. "If I put the candle into this
lantern," he thought, "they will follow it. I will
take them to the hollow place between the roots
of the beech tree where I found the eggs. There
I will leave them. Whomever the Goblins belong
to will be sure to find them."

Six Goblins crowded round to see him take the
candle and put it into the lantern. Six Goblins

never took their eyes off the light. They did not wink, they did not blink—they just stared at the light in the queerest way.

The Woodman went out into the night.

The Goblins stumbled after, their eyes peering at the light ahead. Sometimes one stumbled and fell, but got up again, and went bumping on as before. On they went through the dark woods. Shadows danced about their path, twigs crackled under their feet, and now and then a thud was heard as a Goblin stumbled over a root or a stone.

At last the Woodman found the beech tree. He hung the lantern on a broken branch. The little Goblins sat on the ground in a circle, staring up at the lantern. They did not wink, they did not blink.

But the Woodman turned away and walked into the black night along the tangled path. Branches struck him in the face; one scratched his hand as he tried to thrust it aside. Finally he slipped and fell. He tried to crawl forward, but something seized him by the belt. He gave a scream of terror. It was only the limb of a tree, but the poor man was almost frightened out of his wits.

He looked back at the light, and at the little Goblins sitting there, still and quiet. When he looked away from the light, the darkness seemed even more terrible. Every dark shadow frightened him.

He looked back at the light again, and it seemed as if he were being drawn back to the Goblins. The more he looked at their faces, the more he wanted to be there with them beside the light. Slowly he crawled back towards the circle.

He took his place beside the six Goblins.

Now he found his eyes could not leave the light. His eyes grew big and round, and he stared and stared and stared, at the eerie glow. He did not wink, he did not blink.

And if the light still burns in that dark wood, seven Goblins are sitting under the crooked beech tree—staring and staring at the flickering glow of a candle. They do not wink, they do not blink.

The Wonderful Cat
of Cobbie Bean

BY BARBEE OLIVER CARLETON

I<small>N THE EARLY DAYS</small> of this country there lived by
the sea a ne'er-do-well lad named Cobbie Bean.

In those days witches were said to be abroad in the land. So strange things happened by night and by day, and this is how it was.

From his cornfield on the hill, Cobbie could look out over all the world. He could see the village of Salem, with the forest dark on one side and the harbor bright on the other. He could see the fine ships of his cousin, Captain Bean, who was as fat as a pudding.

Now, the captain was a getter. He got and he got. Already he had got himself a fleet of ships and a wharf and a warehouse; and day by day he got more and more.

And Cobbie could see the handsome house of his other cousin, the famous Deacon Bean, who was as thin as a bone. The deacon was a doer. He did and he did. He wrote deep books that nobody understood. He preached dark sermons that frightened folk half to death. So the deacon was the most famous man in all of Essex County, just as the captain was the richest.

As for Cobbie Bean, he had done nothing, and he had got nothing. Yet, he had the sun at his head and the world at his feet and the merriest heart in the county. He had it all for keeping a cow and a patch of corn. "Nothing to it," said Cobbie Bean.

But one night something happened. It was twilight, and the air was sweet with lilacs and the twittering of birds. Happy as a clam at high tide, Cobbie sat on his doorstep eating his supper of porridge.

Then he saw two figures on horseback, moving with purpose up the hill. One was as fat as a pudding. One was as thin as a bone. And they looked grim, even from a distance.

Cobbie sighed. "I wish my cousins would move to China!" he told himself. Then his Conscience bothered him.

"They only want you to make something of yourself," said his Conscience.

"I doubt it," said Cobbie. "The less I am, the bigger they feel."

"How can you think such a thing!" said his Conscience. "Especially when you didn't lay a hand to the hoe all day."

"I did so," said Cobbie uneasily. The cousins were getting nearer.

"You did not," argued his Conscience. "All morning you lay on your back on the top of the hill and watched the clouds go by. Whistling, at that!"

Cobbie said, "Well, I was wondering . . ."

"Wondering what?" demanded his Conscience. "How to grow a corn crop?"

"I was wondering where the wind goes. . . ."

His Conscience sniffed. "That is all very well. But here come your cousins. Let's see you whistle your way out of this one, Cobbie Bean."

Solemnly, the deacon and the captain hitched their horses to Cobbie's gate. In all their finery, they swept into the cottage and sat stiffly on the two rude stools.

The deacon wrinkled his long, thin nose, as if he smelled something unpleasant. "Well, Cobbie Bean, I see that things are as bad as ever with you."

"Better than ever, Cousin," grinned Cobbie. "Spring is here!"

"Spring!" The captain snorted so loudly that all his five chins jiggled. "Look at those rags you wear, Cobbie Bean. Look at this hut you live in.

35

Look at that cold porridge you eat for your supper." The captain shuddered.

"But I'm happy the way I am," Cobbie said timidly.

"That," hissed the deacon, "is the whole point. Happiness is a sin! If you are happy, Cobbie Bean, it is because you are bewitched!"

Cobbie's eyes popped. "B-bewitched?"

"Bewitched!" thundered the captain. "Your cousin and I agree that the time has come to tell you."

The deacon leaned forward and pointed his bony finger. "Cobbie Bean," he said darkly, "a strange thing happened at your christening. Just as the minister spoke your name, a large, gray cat leaped upon the window ledge. She wore a black cloak and a high-crowned hat, and her eyes glittered like ice! Then she spoke in the voice of the wind, or of the sea, and it filled the meeting-house: 'Cobbie Bean . . . Cobbie Bean . . . I give thee the gift of happiness. . . .'"

Cobbie turned as red as joe-pye weed. The deacon had always taught how sinful it was to be merry. The captain had told all over Salem that men who got ahead had no time for happiness.

"'Gift of happiness,' indeed!" The deacon's long lip curled. "The cat was a witch, of course! As we tried to seize her, she disappeared in a sizzling chain of lightning!"

"And a thunderclap that made us all but deaf!" added the captain in a shaking voice.

"If you would have gifts," preached the deacon scornfully, "you should have the gift of doing. Look at me. I've done and I've done, and now, behold! I am the most famous man in all the county of Essex!"

"How about the gift of getting?" shouted the captain. "I've got and I've got, and look at me now! The richest man in the county!"

"But I had no choice," said poor Cobbie. "I was only a baby!"

"You're not a baby now," snapped the deacon. "You are a do-nothing, living off a cornpatch."

Hopefully, Cobbie said, "Yesterday I did something. I took some fresh herbs down to the jailer, who has the mumps."

The two cousins laughed aloud. "And, pray,"

said the captain, "what did this great deed get you?"

Cobbie bit his fingernail. "Just made us happy, me and the jailer."

"You see?" breathed the deacon. "He has certainly been bewitched!"

"Without a doubt," whispered the captain.

The two cousins looked nervously about them. Night was falling, and Cobbie's cabin was filled with shadows. It was no place to be with a person who was bewitched. They hurried outside and mounted their horses.

"Cobbie Bean," warned the deacon, when he was safely in his saddle, "see that you make something of yourself."

"Before it's too late!" bellowed the captain. And away they trotted down the hill toward Salem.

Poor Cobbie stared after them. Was he bewitched? Nonsense! "Anyway, they're right about one thing," he told his Conscience sadly. "I'm a do-nothing, all right. I didn't even hoe down the cornfield today!" And Cobbie Bean made for the hilltop to hoe a row or two by moonlight.

" 'The gift of happiness!' Pooh!" He struck the

earth such a mighty blow that the hoe caught in the roots of a hobblebush growing at the edge of the field. Like a good farmer, Cobbie seized his axe to chop it down. But its twisting branches and its snowy blossoms made so handsome a picture in the moonlight, that Cobbie grew weak with happiness. Besides, he had heard that a hobblebush holds all sorts of magic. Slowly, he lowered his axe and turned to go home.

Then it happened. Alone in the moonlight, Cobbie heard something more than the peepers in the marsh below. He heard a strange voice whisper, "Cobbie Bean . . . Cobbie Bean . . ." It was the voice of the wind or of the sea. But there was no wind at all that night. Nor could the sound of the sea be heard from Cobbie's lonely hill. Under the hobblebush there was nothing but moon-shadow. Cobbie felt the hair prickle on his neck.

The voice rose from the hobblebush tree and filled the air between earth and heaven like the pealing of bells: "Cobbie Bean . . . Cobbie Bean. . . . Stranger things will come to pass than you have ever seen. . . ."

The voice died away among the hills. For a

moment the tree tossed violently as if in a windstorm. Then there was only the moonlight, flowing peacefully over hobblebush and cornfield.

Cobbie took to his heels. His axe went one way, his hoe the other. Down the hill he sprinted with his shadow close behind. He pounded across the footbridge where the mist reached after him with wet fingers. He burst into his hut and bolted the door and leaned against it, panting.

But he was not alone. There on the stool, full in the moonlight, sat a large, gray cat. She wore a black cloak and a high-crowned hat, and her eyes glittered like ice!

COBBIE BEAN stared at the cat and the cat glared back at Cobbie with eyes that glittered in the moonlight. Cobbie opened his mouth to say "Scat!" but he could only hiss in a jiggly sort of way. He was shaking like the hobblebush he had just fled. After all, it isn't every day that a fellow runs home from a voice in a tree to find in his house a strange cat wearing a cloak and hat!

Cobbie decided to leave. Keeping his eyes on the cat's—for, truly, he could not look away—he

moved the bolt, very slowly. Very softly, he lifted the latch.

"Stop that," the Cat said calmly.

Startled, Cobbie dropped the latch with a clatter.

"Now, come over here," directed the Cat, "and stop acting like those two ninnies you have for cousins."

Cobbie swallowed, and made a wide circle around his guest.

"People!" chuckled the Cat. "Nothing but a bunch of nerves. Here, you might hang up my things before you sit down."

Cobbie Bean took the small cloak and the steeple-crowned hat as one would take up a white-hot poker. He hung them on a peg by the door and seated himself gingerly across the table from the stranger. Finally he cleared his throat. "You can talk!" he croaked.

"So can you!" said the Cat with relief. "I was beginning to wonder if you did anything but hiss. It would be dull to stay with someone who hissed all the time."

"S-stay?" stammered Cobbie. "Did you s-say 's-stay'?"

"There you go hissing again," said the Cat. "And I did say 'stay.'"

Cobbie blinked. "S-stay here?"

"Where else?" asked the Cat.

"But what will folks say?"

The Cat's laugh was like the chiming of bells. "They'd say I am a witch, naturally. And they would hang you for witchcraft, of course. So you must never tell a soul that I am anything but an ordinary cat."

Speechless, Cobbie shook his head.

"And now, Cobbie Bean, I should like my supper. It has been a long journey." The large, gray cat gazed at Cobbie with eyes as chilly as the northeast wind.

Cobbie Bean shivered. He served the porridge with a shaky hand, placing it carefully on the hearth.

His guest sniffed. "On the table, Cobbie Bean. Do you take me for a common cat?"

Cobbie hastened to place the bowl on the table, along with a wooden spoon. The Cat ate with the

43

grace of a queen, but when she was done she wrinkled her nose.

"Porridge. Wooden spoons. We shall have to do better than that."

"Yes, ma'am," said Cobbie humbly.

"Still, thanks to me," the Cat went on dryly, "you do have the gift of happiness, surely the greatest gift on earth."

"Yes, ma'am," said Cobbie, blushing. "Thank you, ma'am."

"Oh, I know what those cousins of yours think about happiness! They do and they get, but they will leave the world just the way they found it. You, Cobbie Bean, have a gift to share. You can make the world a happier place. People are funny. They listen only to their betters."

Cobbie nodded doubtfully.

"In short, Cobbie Bean," said the Cat briskly, "if you are to make the world happier, you must first turn into a gentleman!"

Alarmed, Cobbie bit his fingernail. "But I don't know how."

"Fingers out of your mouth!" ordered the Cat.

44

"I'll teach you, of course. And after that, I shall bewitch you again."

Cobbie moved hastily toward the door.

"Oh, go sit down," said his guest. "I don't mean the turn-you-into-a-mouse sort of bewitching. I do that all the time." To prove it, the Cat suddenly took the shape of a mouse.

"I can do people, too," she said. And there, in place of the mouse, sat the captain, stroking his five chins. Immediately after, the captain gave way to the deacon, stiff as a ramrod and pointing a long finger straight at Cobbie. Then there sat the Cat again, not even breathing hard.

She shrugged. "Low-grade witchcraft. Nothing to it. Making you rich and famous is just as easy. I can do that overnight. But turning you into a gentleman," the Cat looked Cobbie over carefully, "will take a little longer."

And that was the way the magic began. Each day the Cat stayed with Cobbie Bean. Each night she returned to the hobblebush. "Where do you think the magic comes from, eh, Cobbie?" she said, winking broadly.

As the warm summer days went by, the Cat

taught Cobbie how to act kindly and speak gently, and how to live with love toward his fellows. "Think high," said the Cat. "That makes it easy."

And since no true gentleman lacks wisdom, she told him where the birds go in winter and what makes the wind blow, and the tide move, and people do as they do. On the golden afternoons when the corn waved high, Cobbie and the Cat lay side by side on the hilltop. They watched the captain's ships, like great, white birds on a blue wind, sail off to far corners of the earth. Then the Cat told Cobbie wonderful tales about other countries and other times, and a great friendship grew between them.

But sometimes, listening, Cobbie felt a shiver go up his spine. For the voice of the Cat seemed not to be a voice at all. At times it was the night wind blowing. At times it was the sea, hushing into a cove. The Cat must be very wise, and very, very old. Or the Cat must really be, as the cousins had said, a witch!

One day Cobbie dared to ask, "Cat, how is it that you, being—er, what you are, can talk?"

The Cat looked back at him with the gaze of an

old idol. She glanced at the hobblebush. "Magic," she said. "The world's full of it."

And Cobbie was left still wondering if his friend was, after all, a witch. Yet, it seemed that he had never been without the Cat's wisdom. The days when he had put off his hoeing to whistle at the clouds seemed far away. For after Cobbie had learned to think high and act the part of a gentleman, the Cat said, "Now you must learn to work well, or all I have taught you will come to nothing." She showed Cobbie how to plan his time and use his strength so cleverly that he could farm better than before and still have time to study the world around him.

And all this time, the two cousins, through the captain's spyglass, kept an eye on Cobbie's hill. Amazed, they saw Cobbie busily hoeing and busily weeding, and they saw his corn grow like magic!

"I guess that talk of ours did him a world of good," declared the captain.

"Maybe," said the deacon. "Maybe not."

Then one day, when the corn was beginning to tassle, the Cat turned to Cobbie a little sadly. "You are ready now," she told him. "You have learned to think high and to work well. Tonight at midnight, if there is a ring around the moon, come with your cow to the hobblebush. We'll make the world a happier place, all right! And while we're about it, we'll make those cousins of yours pipe a different tune!"

"Cat," said Cobbie, touching her fur fondly, "thank you."

The Cat gazed at him with frosty eyes. "You're welcome. Only beware, Cobbie Bean. Never tell a living soul where the magic comes from!" Then, in a blinding flash of lightning that ringed her round and round, and with a thunderclap that echoed after her through the hills, she disappeared.

A low wind blew in from the sea and the hill was filled with shadows. At the end of the cornfield, the hobblebush began to whisper and toss. His scalp prickling, Cobbie sprang to his feet and sprinted down the hill as if the devil himself were after him. Across the bridge he raced and into the hut, and shot the bolt. Half-afraid, half-hopeful, Cobbie looked about him for the large, gray cat. But the cottage was empty.

Slowly, the night drew out of the sea and lowered over Salem. A dark wind sent clouds racing down the sky. The pale moon rose, like a circle of silk. Higher and higher it climbed, until Cobbie Bean could see full and clear the great ring of light around it!

Then he left for the hilltop, pulling the cow by her halter. His hands were icy and his heart pounded as he picked his way past the boulders and the stiff forms of junipers. Had he taken a witch for his teacher? Would the devil come for him tonight, up here in the full of the moon? The wind rushed past him in a panic. Ahead crouched the hobblebush, like a giant spider. Cobbie's throat was dry, and his tongue felt too large for his mouth. Fearfully, he tied the cow to a branch of the hobblebush.

Then it happened, the thing he was waiting for. A cloud covered the moon. An icy mist rose from the hill, and the hobblebush tossed wildly. As Cobbie stared, the cow bellowed in fear and fell to the ground. Then came the voice that Cobbie remembered. First it was soft like the sea. Then it filled the air like the chant of a winter wind. "Cobbie Bean . . . Cobbie Bean . . . Never tell what you have seen. . . ."

A wailing of voices rose to fill the night. It was a witches' Sabbath! Stiff with fright and cold, Cobbie saw tall figures swirling slowly in the mist. Chanting, they moved like shadows around the hobblebush, each in turn casting something underneath its branches.

"Blood of bat and bone of cat,
  Tongue of frog and tooth of rat,
  Hog's hair, claw of bear,
  Three times three, now follow me. . . ."

Faster and faster they whirled and louder they shrieked, until Cobbie's head reeled. Then, quite suddenly, the wind died. The mist rolled back into the earth, taking the shadowy shapes along with it. The tossing branches came to rest.

Unbelieving, Cobbie Bean stared at the ground beneath the hobblebush.

COBBIE BEAN'S eyes all but popped from his head. In place of his cow stood a splendid black steed, bridled and saddled and pawing the ground. Over a branch of the hobblebush hung a fine suit of clothes, and on the grass lay bags bulging with gold.

"Cat," breathed Cobbie, "wherever you are, listen to me. I don't care if you are a witch! You're a good witch, anyway." Then, never forgetting that he was to make the world happier, he changed his rags for the finery. He filled his saddlebags with gold. Then he leaped into the saddle and set off for Salem.

Like a golden ribbon, the path wound down the rocky hill to the village and the bright harbor. The rising sun touched the junipers with fire. It brought sparks out of every boulder.

"Magic," breathed Cobbie Bean, trotting a little faster.

He passed the meetinghouse where, long ago, the Cat had come to his christening. He began to smell the sea, and the wharf smells of cordage, of tar and of spices. The world was so full of magic that Cobbie joined with the birds in a jolly whistle, for he longed to tell everyone about it.

The good folk of Salem peeped out of their win-

51

dows, or paused at their milking, surprised to see what a gentleman Cobbie Bean had become. All day long his wonderful tune went round in their heads and made the day merry.

Only the two cousins were too busy to listen. After working all night, the deacon was finishing up a book that would frighten the sins right out of folk and make him more famous than ever. And down on the wharf, the captain had been thundering at his men since cockcrow. Doing and getting, the two cousins had no time for tunes.

Suddenly, Cobbie's horse stopped before a splendid new house. It had many steep gables and windows of glass cut in the shape of diamonds. A servant with frosty eyes bowed low at the door. "Welcome home, Master."

Closing the door behind him, the servant turned at once into the large, gray cat. She winked solemnly. "Quite a job of witchcraft, eh, Cobbie?" And she showed him over his house with its fine furnishings and its stores of food, its servants and gardens and coaches and horses.

Cobbie was bewildered. "Is it a dream?"

The Cat's laugh rang out like the chiming of

bells. "No more a dream than the rest of life," said she. "Here your happiness will be no greater than on your hill. But you can share it better."

And Cobbie did. Wherever he went, the people of Salem were the happier for Cobbie Bean. He made the old feel young with his wonderful tales of faraway times and places. He made the sick feel well again with his secrets about how the grass grows and where the wind goes. And sometimes at night, the poor would find at their door a bag of gold or a sack of food. "Cobbie Bean," they would tell each other, blessing him in their hearts.

With the lads in town, Cobbie was a favorite. "You never worry," they told him, "about saving people's souls or getting more money than anybody else. Yet, you're happy and successful. Tell us your secret, Cobbie," they begged.

"It's easy," he laughed. "Think high. Work well. Pass your happiness along."

And so they did, laughing and singing at their tasks and working as never before. Only now and then people wondered. "Who told these marvelous things to Cobbie Bean?" they asked each other.

But Cobbie only smiled. For he knew that

· magic was thought evil, and that witchcraft was punished by death. He would keep his promise to the Cat never to tell where the magic came from.

Nor did Cobbie himself forget what the Cat had taught him. Thinking high and working well, he became in time as rich and famous as he was beloved.

Now his two cousins did not know what to make of all this. "Perhaps he has some secret," whispered the deacon, "about how to become rich and famous."

"After all we have done for that ne'er-do-well," blustered the captain, "he should be made to share it with us!"

So, with canes tapping on the cobbles, off they trotted to learn how Cobbie Bean had become richer and more famous than they.

Once at Cobbie's house, they roared at the servant who led them to the study. Brutally, they kicked at the large, gray cat that came to greet them. "If I didn't know better," hissed the deacon, "I'd say that was the same beast that came to the christening!"

54

"Hush," said the captain, as Cobbie entered, wearing the fine garb of a gentleman.

"Well, Cobbie Bean," purred the deacon. "We see that you have come up in the world."

"That I have," smiled Cobbie, remembering his promise to the Cat.

"But, Cobbie," added the captain shrewdly, "we hardly expected this much profit from our advice. Have you some secret, perhaps, to share with us?"

"I have, Cousins," said Cobbie earnestly. "Think high. Work well. Pass your happiness along."

But the deacon squinted darkly into Cobbie's soul. "Cobbie Bean, you are not telling the whole truth. There's more to this than meets the eye!"

Cobbie shuffled his feet. Before he could think of an answer, the Cat silently walked into the room on all fours, like any common cat. She leaped into a chair and stared at the cousins with eyes like the northeast wind. They shook with cold and tried to look away. But the eyes of the cat held them stiff and frost-bound. Finally, with teeth chattering, they left the room as fast as shaking legs could carry them.

The two looked so miserable that Cobbie followed them to the door. "Wait!" he said. Surely, as long as he kept the Cat's secret, he might tell about the hobblebush.

He whispered swiftly, "Go to the hobblebush on the hill when there's a ring around the moon."

Scarcely able to hide their delight, the two cousins took their leave.

That very night there came a pale circle around the moon that half-filled the heavens. Two figures, one as fat as a pudding, one as thin as a bone, rode stealthily up Cobbie's lonely hill. Soon they reached the hobblebush.

"This must be the place," whispered the deacon nervously.

The captain rubbed his fat hands together. "Now for the gifts that will make us as rich and famous as Cobbie Bean."

"Hark!" cried the deacon. "Is that the wind?"

Startled, the two saw the branches begin to toss. They felt a chill rushing of wind and saw a gray mist rise around the hobblebush. They heard a voice that rode the wind like the tolling of a bell. "Cobbie Bean . . . told. . . . Cobbie Bean . . . told. . . ."

Then the night was filled with the wailing of voices and the swirling of dark figures. The cousins stared like statues, as faster and dizzier whirled the shapes. Then straight toward the two on horseback they came, screaming and scratching and pounding and beating. The wretched pair threw their arms over their heads. Plunging in terror, their horses turned into squealing pigs that bore them pell-mell down the hill, beaten and battered and bleeding and tattered.

"Witchcraft!" gasped the deacon as they galloped into Salem.

Straight to the house of the magistrate they rode. Pounding on the door, they got that gentleman out of bed and told him their story.

"So Cobbie Bean can't be our cousin at all," finished the deacon. "If his cat is a witch, then he must be a witch himself!"

Horrified, the magistrate threw on his clothes. With trembling legs, the three crept down the dark street. They peered through the window into Cobbie Bean's study, where a candle still burned.

There sat Cobbie before his fire, looking handsome and scholarly in his fine clothes. Opposite him in a high-backed chair sat the great, gray cat, still in her cap and cloak. Her strange voice filled the room with the sound of the wind and the sea.

"You broke your promise, Cobbie Bean," the Cat was saying sadly. "And now, evil will come of it."

"*Witchcraft!*" gasped the magistrate, with every hair on end.

"*Witchcraft!*" nodded the cousins.

"Cobbie Bean!" called the magistrate in a shaking voice. "*In the name of the Governor of Massachusetts Bay, I arrest you for witchcraft!*"

POOR COBBIE BEAN was as damp as a mushroom. He sat on the jail floor with a chain around his leg. There was not a window in the place, but Cobbie knew by the nearby crowing of a cock that the night had run out. Now they would come and take him away to be hanged for witchcraft.

Cobbie shivered and tightened his belt. Hanging is not a pleasant thought on an empty stomach.

"Oh, Cat," moaned Cobbie for the hundredth

time. "I'm sorry I told about the hobblebush. If you are really magic, help me now!"

But the Cat did not appear. All through the dark days of Cobbie's trial, the Cat had not come, either by day or night. Now, as then, there was only the *drip, drip,* of water down the dungeon wall. For a long time, Cobbie thought of their golden hours together on the hilltop above the sea, where even now the gallows tree was waiting.

Suddenly, a key grated in the lock. In came his friend, the jailer, looking so miserable that Cobbie felt sorry for him. "Here, take my hanky," said Cobbie.

"I can't help it," sniffled the jailer, unlocking Cobbie's chain. "You were so good to me when I had the mumps." At the thought, he buried his face in Cobbie's hanky and sobbed.

The magistrate waited at the front door to tie Cobbie's hands behind his back. Under his eyes were circles the size of saucers. "I haven't slept a wink all night," he said, with his lip quivering. "You cheered up the town so nicely, Cobbie, I still don't see how you can be a witch. I'm all mixed up."

"So am I, sir," said Cobbie. "But you must do your duty." With that, Cobbie led the way out into the sunlight. The dew sparkled on the grass. The sparrows twittered in the trees. The bright air was filled with the smell of the tide and the bayberry growing on the beach. Cobbie sniffed deeply. It was a wonderful world, and this was his last morning in it!

There stood the militia, as colorful as a quilt. Behind them the cart waited, with a tired old horse to draw it. The deacon and the captain sat on horseback at either side. They sat rather painfully, and their horses were brand-new. Behind the cart waited the people of Salem, silent and sad. But nowhere in all that staring crowd was the familiar, furry face with the eyes of ice.

"You broke your promise, Cobbie Bean," the Cat had said that night of his arrest. "And now, evil will come of it."

Cobbie bowed his head and climbed into the cart. "Serves me right," he muttered. "After all you did for me, I had to go break my promise."

The drum started its slow, deep, beat, beat, beat. The jailer blew his nose and pulled the old horse forward. *Clop, clop,* Cobbie bounced over the cobbles, with the people of Salem following behind. They were the old and the ill and the poor and the young, whom Cobbie had made happy. And at the very end walked the hangman, all in black. No one would speak to him, and he was feeling very sorry for himself.

Slowly, the procession wound up the hill, behind the magistrate on his white horse. At the very top rose the gallows, dark against the sky. Nearby stood the hobblebush. But the Cat was nowhere at all.

Maybe, thought poor Cobbie, it was all a wonderful dream. And this is the nightmare ending.

Up rode the magistrate, splendid in his red cloak. "Cobbie Bean!" he called. "Come forward."

Cobbie climbed down from the cart and mounted the steps to the gallows. The minister read a prayer. There was a long roll of the drums. The hangman stood waiting.

Then the crowd broke their silence. "Witches are evil!" cried one. "But Cobbie Bean is the best lad in town!"

"Witches hurt people!" cried another. "But Cobbie has helped every one of us!"

"Witches are full of woe!" called a third. "But Cobbie is the happiest lad in Salem!"

"Silence!" shouted the magistrate in a quavering voice. "I feel the same way. But Cobbie Bean will not confess, and we must do our duty. Hangman, carry on." Then the poor magistrate rode off behind the hobblebush to have a good cry.

Cobbie looked his last at the sky. A little breeze sprang up, and the hobblebush started to toss. But then the blindfold was tied on, tickling his nose. The hangman placed the rope around his neck.

The wind began to blow so cold that the people hugged themselves to keep warm. It blew so high that it sounded like the wailing of a giant cat. An icy mist rose up from the hill.

Back rode the magistrate with his scarlet cloak billowing behind. "Cobbie Bean . . . Have you anything to say before you die?"

Amazed, the townspeople looked at one another. The magistrate's voice sounded quite different. It sounded like the wind itself, or like the sea. His eyes, too, looked strange. They were frosty and cold, like eyes of ice. The people shivered and tried to peer through the mist. Some said later that it seemed not to be the magistrate at all, but rather, a large, gray cat.

Cobbie Bean took hope. "Not guilty, sir!" he cried.

At that, the magistrate threw back his head and laughed. His laugh sounded like the chiming of bells, and it filled the very heavens. "Not guilty? Why, then, there has been a mistake! Hangman, set Cobbie Bean free!"

The people cheered as the hangman hastened to obey.

"Go back to your homes, good people!" shouted the magistrate. "And let's have no more foolishness about witchcraft. Remember, the world is full of magic, and most of it is good!"

Again the people cheered.

But a loud voice rose above the wind. "I object!" It was the deacon, looking as dreadful as he knew how.

"And so do I!" thundered the captain, his five chins shaking with rage.

The magistrate turned to where the captain and the deacon sat astride their new horses. He fixed his icy eyes upon them and said in a terrible voice, "*Scat!*"

Now what happened next may not be so. It is difficult to see, with the wind in your eyes. But some said that the horses turned into pigs and ran squealing down the hill, with the deacon and the captain hanging on for dear life. As far as anybody knows, they kept on going all the way to China, for never again were the cousins seen in Salem, from that day to this.

The wind blew like a hurricane, and the townspeople ran for home. It blew so hard that the gallows tree toppled and fell onto the hobblebush, carrying it to the ground, along with Cobbie and the magistrate.

At that, the wind stopped as suddenly as it had started. The sun shone warm on the hill, and the birds sang again in the trees.

Cobbie crept out of the wreckage and helped the magistrate to his feet.

"What happened?" asked the magistrate in his usual voice and with his eyes as red as before.

"The wind blew the gallows down, sir," explained Cobbie.

"So it did," frowned the magistrate, feeling the bump on his head. "I seem to have forgotten what happened after I rode back here to—er, blow my nose."

"You came back and set me free," said Cobbie.

The magistrate brightened. "I did, did I? Good for me! That's the smartest thing I ever did in my life. Well, good day to you, Cobbie Bean."

And the magistrate rode off down the hill, rubbing his head.

Frantically, Cobbie looked through the wreckage. "Cat," he whispered, "where are you?"

There lay his cat under a branch of the fallen hobblebush. Cobbie freed her and held her on his lap. Her eyes were open, but Cobbie could see that the frost was leaving them.

"Oh, Cat, you are dying," cried Cobbie.

"Don't be silly," said the Cat. "Magic never dies." She winked solemnly at Cobbie. But her voice was getting weaker.

"What do you think of that show we just put on, eh, Cobbie?"

"It was wonderful, Cat," said Cobbie warmly. "Thank you very much."

"Don't mention it," whispered the Cat. With the last of her voice she reminded Cobbie of something important to ordinary cats. "Fish . . ." she gasped, "for breakfast . . . cream . . . for supper. . . ." Now the frost had gone entirely. She looked at Cobbie with the hungry eyes of any ordinary cat.

"Then home we go to breakfast," said Cobbie Bean, blinking his eyes very fast. The Cat had given her magic to save him. The hobblebush was gone. Now, to the end of her days, she would be nothing but a common cat, a large, gray cat, that loved him very much.

He lifted her tenderly into the cart, where she curled up in his lap. Before they were halfway down the hill, the cat had closed her eyes and was purring splendidly.

Cobbie looked out to where the sea and the sky came together. "I won't forget you, Cat," he whispered. And he never did forget.

In a few years' time, Cobbie married a fine girl in Salem. Never did he tire of telling his children, and later on his grandchildren, the story about his wonderful cat.

And the people of Salem have not forgotten. To this very day, whenever the moon is full and the wind howls and the sea is running high on the beach, they remember that the world is filled with magic.

"Listen!" they tell one another. "It's the wonderful cat of Cobbie Bean, going by on the wind."

Teeny-Tiny

BY JOSEPH JACOBS

O<small>NCE</small> <small>UPON</small> <small>A</small> <small>TIME</small> there was a teeny-tiny woman who lived in a teeny-tiny house in a teeny-tiny village.

Now, one day this teeny-tiny woman put on her teeny-tiny bonnet, and went out of her teeny-tiny house to take a teeny-tiny walk. And when this teeny-tiny woman had gone a teeny-tiny way, she came to a teeny-tiny gate; so the teeny-tiny woman opened the teeny-tiny gate, and went into a teeny-tiny churchyard.

And when this teeny-tiny woman had got into the teeny-tiny churchyard, she saw a teeny-tiny bone on a teeny-tiny grave, and the teeny-tiny woman said to her teeny-tiny self, "This teeny-tiny bone will make me some teeny-tiny soup for my teeny-tiny supper."

So the teeny-tiny woman put the teeny-tiny bone into her teeny-tiny pocket, and went home to her teeny-tiny house.

Now when the teeny-tiny woman got home to her teeny-tiny house, she was a teeny-tiny bit tired; so she went up to her teeny-tiny stairs to her teeny-tiny bed, and put the teeny-tiny bone into a teeny-tiny cupboard. And when this teeny-tiny woman had been to sleep a teeny-tiny time, she was awakened by a teeny-tiny voice from the teeny-tiny cupboard, which said:

"Give me my bone!"

And this teeny-tiny woman was a teeny-tiny frightened, so she hid her teeny-tiny head under the teeny-tiny clothes and went to sleep again. And when she had been to sleep again a teeny-tiny time, the teeny-tiny voice again cried out from the teeny-tiny cupboard a teeny-tiny louder,

"Give me my bone!"

This made the teeny-tiny woman a teeny-tiny more frightened, so she hid her teeny-tiny head a teeny-tiny further under the teeny-tiny clothes. And when the teeny-tiny woman had been to sleep again a teeny-tiny time, the teeny-tiny voice from the teeny-tiny cupboard said again a teeny-tiny louder,

"Give me my bone!"

And this teeny-tiny woman was a teeny-tiny bit more frightened, but she put her teeny-tiny head out of the teeny-tiny clothes, and said in her loudest teeny-tiny voice,

"TAKE IT!"

71

The Conjure Wives

BY FRANCES G. WICKES

Once upon a time when a Halloween night
came on the dark o' the moon, a lot o' old conjure

72

wives was a-sittin' by the fire an' a-cookin' a big supper for theirselves.

The wind was a-howlin' round like it does on Halloween nights, an' the old conjure wives they hitched theirselves up to the fire an' talked about the spells they was a-goin' to weave long come midnight.

By an' by there come a-knockin' at the door.

"Who's there?" called an old conjure wife. "Who-o? Who-o?"

"One who is hungry and cold," said a voice.

Then the old conjure wives, they all burst out laughin' an' they called out:

>"We's a-cookin' for ourselves.
>Who'll cook for you?
>Who? Who?"

The voice didn't say nothin', but the knockin' just kept on.

"Who's that a-knockin'?" called out another conjure wife. "Who? Who?"

Then there come a whistlin', wailin' sound:

"Let me in, do-o-o-o!
 I'se cold thro-o-o-o an' thro-o-o-o,
 An' I'se hungry too-o-o!"

Then the old conjure wives, they all burst out laughin', an' they commenced to sing out:

"Git along, do!
 We's a-cookin' for ourselves.
 Who'll cook for you?
 Who? Who?"

The voice didn't say nothin', but the knockin' just kept on.

The old conjure wives they went to work a-cookin' of the supper for theirselves, an' the voice didn't say nothin', but the knockin' just kept on.

An' then the old conjure wives they hitched up to the fire an' they ate an' they ate—an' the voice didn't say nothin', but the knockin' just kept on. An' the old conjure wives they called out again:

"Go way, do!
 We's a-cookin' for ourselves
 Who'll cook for you?
 Who? Who?"

An' the voice didn't say nothin', but the knockin' just kept on.

Then the old conjure wives began to get scared-like, an' one of 'em says, "Let's give it somethin' an' get it away before it spoils our spells."

An' the voice didn't say nothin', but the knockin' just kept on.

Then the old conjure wives they took the littlest piece of dough, as big as a pea, an' they put it in the fry pan.

An' the voice didn't say nothin', but the knockin' just kept on.

An' when they put the dough in the fry pan it begun to swell an' swell, an' it swelled over the fry pan an' it swelled over the top o' the stove an' it swelled out on the floor.

An' the voice didn't say nothin', but the knockin' just kept on.

Then the old conjure wives got scared an' they ran for the door, an' the door was *shut tight*.

An' the voice didn't say nothin', but the knockin' just kept on.

An' then the dough it swelled an' it swelled all over the floor an' it swelled up into the chairs. An' the old conjure wives they climbed up on the backs of the chairs an' they were scareder and scareder. An' they called out, "Who's that a-knockin' at the door? Who? Who?"

An' the voice didn't say nothin', but the knockin' just kept on.

An' the dough kept a-swellin' an' a-swellin', an' the old conjure wives begun to scrooge up smaller an' smaller, an' their eyes got bigger an' bigger with scaredness, an' they kept-a-callin', "Who's that a-knockin'? Who? Who?"

An' then the knockin' stopped, and the voice called out,

"Fly out the window, do!
There's no more house for you!"

An' the old conjure wives they spread their wings an' they flew out the windows an' off into the woods, all a-callin', "Who'll cook for you? Who? Who?"

An' now if you go into the woods in the dark o' the moon, you'll see the old conjure wife owls an' hear 'em callin', "Who'll cook for you? Who-o! Who-o!"

Only on a Halloween night you don't want to go round the old owls, because *then* they turns to old conjure wives a-weavin' their spells.

Spook's Bones

BY LOUIS C. JONES

T<small>HE BOYS WERE WORKING</small> intently on the tail assembly of the model transport plane. It was well after bedtime, for Pete's folks, when they went out,

78

had told the boys to go upstairs at eight-thirty. Now the clock was striking nine. But the problem of the tail was a tough one and could hardly be left for tomorrow. Besides, Joe didn't come to spend the night often. When they heard the first step on the top stair they hardly noticed it. At the second step Pete spoke up sharply, but without raising his eyes from their task.

"Sis, get back to bed. You know what Mom told you."

The footsteps kept coming slowly down the stairs. It wasn't the weight on the steps that made Pete turn, for that was light enough, but Carol never came down a pair of stairs slowly in her life. And if it wasn't Carol, who was it?

Never before had Pete seen the man who stood there—tall and gaunt, with tanned, knotty hands and a weary stoop to his shoulder. His clothes were ragged and strangely out of date. Pete wasn't scared, just surprised. You couldn't really be scared of a face like this man's. There were kind, sad lines around the mouth and the gray eyes. Pete was still gaping when Joe spoke.

79

"Well, hello, George! So you really came up, did you?"

"Yeah," the man said. "I figured you two would be alone tonight."

"Who is this guy?" Pete asked, still surprised not to see his sister.

"This is George, Pete. I told you all about him on the bus the other day. George, this is Pete."

"I'm mighty glad to meet you 'cause I think you can help me," said George in a hopeful voice.

"Gee, I'd like to help you, George," said Pete. "That is—I guess I would. Are you really—I mean, is it like Joe told me? Are you—?"

"Well, now, Pete, I don't know. I don't know just what Joe told you. If he told you how I used to peddle tin all through this section, and how this was the last farm I ever stopped at, and how I'm needing your help now—I guess he told you right. You see, Pete, I can't rest. I got this thing on my mind all the time. Somebody who lives here now has got to make it right. I figured maybe you were the one."

"Well, gee, George, I guess we can help. Do we have to do it tonight?"

"Well," said George, "there's a good moon to-night."

"How do we start?" asked Joe.

"You go out to that big woodpile—the old woodpile in the back of the barn."

"We haven't touched that woodpile since we moved here four years ago," broke in Pete. Pop cut down so many trees and sawed them up for firewood, we haven't had to use that wood."

"I know that, son," said George, "and nobody else has touched it. All I want you boys to do is go down to the far end of that pile and dig until you come to the place where my tin is buried. Then you'll know you're in the right spot and you keep digging down below that. Then you come to the important thing. . . ."

Pete was listening intently to every word George said. Suddenly he realized that something weird and wonderful was happening. George was disappearing. It was not that he was going away—it was just that when he finished the sentence, he wasn't there. First there had been three of them and now there were only two.

"Whillikers!" said Pete, "I'd somehow forgotten all about his being dead!"

PETE RAN upstairs and got some mittens and a couple of sweaters, because the October air was cold. Both boys walked out the back door and down behind the barn where the full moon shone cold and clear on the old woodpile.

The wood was dry and light. They started at the top and threw pieces off the pile so they fell every which way in the grass.

"This isn't easy!" Pete said slowly.

"But we gotta do it. I promised George that first night I met him."

"How'd you get mixed up in this, Joe?"

"One night, along about nine o'clock, I saw lights in the old Staats house. I knew the Staatses weren't there. Then down the little road between our house and theirs I saw George pacing up and down. 'Course I didn't know he was a—I mean, I thought he was a man. I didn't see any reason to be scared of him, so I says 'Hello' and he says, 'Hello, you're Joe, aren't you?' And I says, 'Yep, I'm Joe. I never saw *you* around before.' So he says, 'No, but I've been watching you—you and Pete.' So I says, 'Do you know Pete?' And he says, 'Nope, but I wish I did. He's about the only one could really help me.' 'What's the matter?' I says to him, and he comes back with 'What I got, the trouble with me, is hard to say. I'm not like you. I been dead, you know, 'most a hundred years.' Well, when he said it like that, Pete, I could have jumped. I heard they come around, of course. Especially at night around the Staats place. But I never talked to one, 'specially not about being a ghost."

Pete was quiet for a minute. Then he said, "I think I would have been scared."

"You weren't scared tonight when George came in," Joe reminded him.

There was a long silence then. The boys were halfway done now. Their hands were getting tired, and they were slowing down.

"When did he tell you, exactly, about this?" Pete asked.

"It was that same night, after I had gone to bed. George came into the room and sat down and told me. It seems that the year this all happened, he was carrying around all the money he had saved up for five years. He was gonna open a little store someplace. He didn't know anybody to take care of the money for him, and he didn't trust banks, so he had it all wadded up in big bills in his pants' pocket. It was winter and he had pretty well sold out all he had. When he started out he had had a horse and cart piled up with tin—pots, pans, and stuff. He was down to four or five pans, and the week before he had had a chance to sell his horse and cart for a good price. He wasn't going to need them when he opened his store so he grabbed the chance and sold out.

"Well, he came to your house along about dusk one night and some new folks had bought the place. There was a man and a woman with the meanest hired man he had ever seen in his life. George asked them could he stay there that night. All he wanted was a place to lay his blanket. They said he could sleep on the floor up in the hired man's room."

"That must be my room now, right?" asked Pete.

"That's the way I figure it. Anyway this hired

84

man didn't like the idea and was mighty crabby about it.

"When they were getting undressed George suddenly sneezed and he pulled his handkerchief out and this big wad of bills came with it. The fellow saw the bills and didn't say much, but after George had got to sleep he had this dream about not being able to breathe. Just as he was waking up, he opened his eyes, and the moonlight was coming right on the face of this great big fellow who was choking the very life out of him. The very life! Yes, sir, George was dead before he knew it.

"Then George stayed around while the hired man picked up his body and very carefully came down those back stairs from your bedroom, down through the kitchen, out in back where this woodpile is—right here where we're sitting. And George says first he took the wood down like we've done now. Then he dug a grave under where the woodpile had been, putting the dirt into bushel baskets. Then he buried George and put the tin that was left on top, covered it over with dirt and piled up the wood again the way it had been. Then he took the dirt that was left and spread it all over the garden. The next morning he just told the folks that the tin man had left at the crack of dawn."

Maybe it was the cold, maybe it was the funny shadows that passed over the moon—but Pete sat on the woodpile, shivering.

"Look, Joe, what do you say we do this some other time? I'm not so sure I want to get mixed up in this."

"You wouldn't let me down now, would you?" came a third voice from the darkness. And there was George, standing there looking at them, sad as he could be.

"Pete, my boy, you don't know what it is to have your body buried off in a forsaken spot like the bottom of a woodpile. A man likes to feel he's buried with people. I can't rest like a man ought to until my bones are taken out of this place and put where they belong."

"What about this hired man, George?" Pete's voice was small.

"Oh, him!" George answered. "It didn't take me long to handle him. Two days after he killed me, he ran away from here, and I followed him. He went out and walked along the railroad track. About two miles from here, a train came pounding down the line and he stepped off the track, but not quite far enough. I gave him a little shove and that was the end of him. It's a bad thing to have a dead man mad at you. It's a worse thing to steal a dead man's money—'specially if it's every cent he's saved for six hard years. I tell you, Pete, I never hurt a single soul as long as I was alive, but I fixed him in my own time."

"He still isn't around by any chance?" Pete asked apprehensively.

"I never saw him," said George. "He never comes down with the others to the Staats place when we have our meetings. No, I never saw him again."

After a pause, he said, "Now what do you say, boys—let's get this done. There isn't much time, you know, before your folks get back."

The boys worked hard and soon they were down to the bare ground. Pete disappeared and came back with a spade and a shovel—and while George watched, they dug.

"Take it easy now. I think you're getting close,"

George cautioned. And, sure enough, pretty soon a bone like the upper part of a man's arm lay in the dirt. Pete got a bushel basket and put it in very gently. Joe kept digging and soon they found another. And another. Finally the skull—clean as it could be once you knocked the soil away. As George watched them carefully putting each piece in the basket, he spoke softly:

"You're very kind to me, boys."

They took the basket and hid it in the haymow in the barn and then came back to fill in the hole just as fast as they could move. Then they piled up the wood again as best they could.

"Boys," George said when they were done, "I want to say again how grateful I am to you, but there's one other little matter. When are you going to rebury me?"

"Well," said Joe. "I thought we'd take you down to that old burying ground outside the Staats place. It would be near the house down there and handy for your parties."

"That's fine," said George, "that's fine. Now, when?"

"Well," said Pete. "I'm going down to Joe's to

88

spend Saturday night and if you wouldn't mind my putting the bones in a bag, I could take them down on my bike when I go. Then we could bury them sometime over the week end."

"Boys, that's just fine. Down there I'll be real happy. If there's anything I can ever do for you, you let me know."

"It's okay," said Joe. "We're glad to help you out."

"Would you—sometime—" broke off Pete, not knowing how to go on.

"What, son? Anything at all."

"Saturday, maybe, would you tell us more about —about some of the ghosts—the other ghosts, I mean?"

For the first time George grinned at them. "You bury me the way I ought to be, and then Saturday we'll get together. How's that?" They were about to answer him, but George had disappeared once more.

Right after breakfast on Saturday Pete was off on his bike for Joe's house. In the basket on his handle bars was a grain bag, neatly folded. It made an irregular shaped package but it weighed so little that he barely realized it was there.

Pete lived two miles or more back from the Hudson, high above the river. Joe lived on an island, separated from the mainland by a longish bridge.

When Pete reached the river road he turned left for a mile, then took a side road leading to the river.

"Hi, Joeyeee." It made a crazy sound as Pete called it.

But back from the barn came, "Hiyi, Pete." And Joe came running.

Five minutes later the two boys were walking rapidly down the little grass-covered wagon track that led to the south end of the island and the old Staats house with its aged cemetery. Each carried a shovel over his shoulder and the bag of bones between them, not because it was heavy, but to share the responsibility.

"George was here last night," said Joe casually.
"Yeah?"

"He told me just where he wants his bones buried. Over near old Jacob Staats in the far corner. Says the old man was a good customer of his and a good friend."

By now they had come to the gateway of the little family burying ground. The boys found Jacob's grave off in its far corner, just as George had told Joe they would, and they began to dig. It was easy going, for the soil was sandy.

"How deep do you think we ought to go?" Pete asked when they were down a couple of feet.

"Six feet is the customary depth," said a voice that made them jump halfway out of their skins.

"Holy Moses, George! I wish you wouldn't scare us so," scolded Joe.

"I thought you had to wait till night, George. Can you come around any— Hey, George, where are you?" Pete was bewildered, for, close as the voice was, there was no George to be seen.

"Pete, my friend," the old man said, "your notions about ghosts are way out of date. Any time of day or night, that's us. Sometimes we 'show' and sometimes we don't; that's up to us. Look!"

And sure enough, after a second or two there he was, as visible as a tree. Then he roared with laughter, slapping his thigh, as he looked at the boys' faces. "There are a lot of silly notions going around about us. As a matter of fact, we can do almost anything we could when we were alive. More things, really. Couldn't disappear when I was alive." And with that he wasn't there any more, just the sound of his laugh as the boys stared at the air where he had been.

"George is feeling a lot more cheerful, isn't he?" Pete observed.

"Told me he felt like a new spirit since we dug him up," Joe said. "He's much more fun than he was."

They dug for a spell, thinking over what they had heard, thinking, too, about the fact that George was there by them, watching. They figured the hole didn't have to be very long or wide. First one would get down and work awhile, then the other. The deeper they went, the harder going it was. When Pete was waist-deep he said, "George, that isn't six feet, but don't you think that's deep enough?"

"We-el, lads, each of you do six more shovelfuls and we'll call it a day. If we don't get it right now, I'll have trouble later. Get it right and I can rest till Judgment Day. When everything is settled up and there are no loose ends, a man can rest. If his conscience is clear, of course."

"Does that really make a difference?" asked Pete.

"Does it! I could tell you stories about friends of mine who will *never* rest, because of the things they can't forget, things that weigh on their minds and will for all eternity."

The boys dug some more. Then they put some pine boughs in the bottom of the grave and laid the bones out. George's voice kept saying how pleased he was, and how grateful. They then put some more pine boughs over the lot of them and began the filling in.

"Do you need any words said, George?" asked Joe.

"Well, now, boy, that's real nice of you to remember. I reckon it would make it more official and there sure weren't any words said last time. You might each think a little prayer or something."

So the boys said a silent prayer apiece and when they raised their heads they looked over the place where the voice had been coming from. Only now

George was standing there again and his face was one great smile.

"That sure was mighty right and nice," he said.

It didn't take them very long to finish the job. They were agreed that it would be better not to put any stones or marker over the spot, since, in the summertime, the Staats family came back once in a while to the burying ground and they might wonder about a new grave. Instead they pulled some vines over the place and piled up some leaves that were blown into a corner. Then they stood back a ways and found that they had done a good job of concealment.

"Let's go ask my mother for some sandwiches and tell her we're going up to the other end of the island to explore. Will you come, George?"

"Today I'll do whatever you lads want me to."

"Tell us about your friends," Pete said. He shivered. "Tell us about the ghosts who will never rest, because of the things they can't forget!"

Which Was Witch?

BY ELEANORE M. JEWETT

T HERE WAS ONCE a wise and learned man named
Kim Su-ik. He lived just inside the south gate of
Seoul but might as well have lived anywhere for

all the thought he gave the matter. His mind was entirely taken up with study and books, and one could say of him, as Im Bang said of another scholar, "He used to awake at first cockcrow, wash, dress, take up his book and never lay it aside. On his right were pictures, on his left were books, and he happy between. He rose to be a Prime Minister."

One night Kim Su-ik was absorbed in studying a Chinese classic when he suddenly felt hungry. He clapped his hands to summon a servant and immediately the door of his room opened.

His wife stepped in.

"What does the master of the house desire?" said she.

"Food," he answered briefly, his attention already returned to the book in his lap.

"I have little in the house but a few roasted chestnuts. If that will suffice I will bring them to you myself. The servants have long since gone to their sleeping quarters."

Kim Su-ik grunted his approval and went on with his studies. In a very short time the door opened again and his wife came in bearing a brass bowl full of hot roasted chestnuts. He helped himself to one and was in the act of putting it into his mouth when once more the door opened and in stepped his wife with a brass bowl full of hot roasted chestnuts.

But his wife was already there, standing beside him with the bowl in her hands!

Kim Su-ik, his mouth still open and a chestnut half in it looked in astonishment from one to the other of the identical women. They were as like as two pins—faces, features, figures, clothes, the way they stood, the way they used their fingers and moved their shoulders. Never were twins more completely alike. Kim Su-ik passed his hands before his eyes. He must have overdone his studying, he thought to himself, read too late and too steadily. His eyes were playing tricks on him, that was all. He was seeing double.

But when he looked again the two women were still there, and what was stranger still, they seemed not to be aware of each other, but stood quietly, gracefully, their eyes fastened on him as if waiting to know his pleasure.

The scholar leaped to his feet, choking back the

cry of terror that rose in his throat. He knew, suddenly, without a doubt what this meant. It was midnight, the moon was at the full, ghosts, evil spirits, witches and goblins would be abroad filled with power.

One of these two creatures standing before him was his wife, known and loved by him all his wedded life and perhaps not quite fully appreciated, he hastily decided. The other must be a witch, able to change into any form she chose in the twinkling of an eye. But which was which? How could he protect his wife and drive this evil double from beside her?

Being a quick thinker as well as a learned one, Kim Su-ik plunged into action. He seized the arm of one of the women with his right hand and before the other could realize what he was about, he had her arm fast in his left hand. They turned mildly reproachful eyes upon him but made no effort to free themselves.

"My dear," said one, "too much study has fevered your brain."

"My dear," said the other, "too much reading of books has affected your mind."

Kim Su-ik looked from one to the other. Not a particle of difference was there to give him a hint as to which was wife and which was witch. He shook them gently. They smiled indulgently as at a child. He shook harder. No resentment, no struggle to get free. He was tempted to relax his grip on the two arms, but he knew he must not for a moment do that and hung on more firmly than ever.

Minutes went by, then hours, the dull slow-moving hours between midnight and cockcrow. The three stood silent, motionless, in the same spot. Kim Su-ik grew weary beyond words. So, too, must his wife be weary, but neither of the two women he held so tightly by the arm said anything or showed by any movement or expression of the face that she was tired, puzzled or angry.

His wife would have been tired and puzzled—angry, too, perhaps, but she would not have blustered or scolded. Any other woman would, were she witch or human. But surely his wife would say something. What in the world had got into her? Was she bewitched? Or walking in her sleep? Perhaps she was not either one of these two women. He wanted to rush into the other part of the house to see if she was there, thus proving that both of these were witches. But he did nothing, just hung on, grimly, silently.

At long last a cock crowed. Immediately the woman at his left tried to wrench her arm free. The other remained quiet. Kim Su-ik dropped the unresisting one and threw all his strength into a struggle with the other. Like a wild thing the creature fought, biting, snarling, spitting, leaping back and forth. Still the scholar held on to her and would not let go. The arm in his hand shrank and grew hairy. The whole figure dwindled, the eyes grew round and green and blazed with fury.

Another cock crowed and another, and the first gray light of dawn melted the dark shadows out of doors. But Kim Su-ik had no thought or time to notice the coming of day. With a hideous shriek the creature changed before his very eyes into a powerful wildcat. In horror he loosed his hold, and she leaped through the window and was gone.

"I still think you are studying too much," said a quiet, familiar voice behind him, and there stood his wife, pale, trembling a little, but smiling confidently.

"Why didn't you let me know which was which?" demanded Kim Su-ik.

His wife laughed. "I don't know what you are talking about. You behaved very strangely, but then, one never knows what to expect of a scholar. Which was which what?"

"Witch!" said Kim Su-ik.

The Water Ghost

BY JOHN KENDRICK BANGS

Tʜᴇ ᴛʀᴏᴜʙʟᴇ ᴡɪᴛʜ Harrowby Hall was that it was haunted, and, what was worse, the ghost did not merely appear at the bedside of a person, but remained there for one mortal hour before it disappeared.

It never appeared except on Christmas Eve, and then as the clock was striking twelve. The owners of Harrowby Hall had tried their hardest to rid themselves of the damp and dewy lady who rose up out of the best bedroom floor at midnight, but they had failed. They had tried stopping the clock, so that the ghost would not know when it was midnight; but she made her appearance just the same, and there she would stand until everything about her was thoroughly soaked.

Then the owners of Harrowby Hall closed up every crack in the floor with hemp, and over this were placed layers of tar and canvas; the walls were made waterproof, and the doors and windows likewise, in the hope that the lady would find it difficult to leak into the room. But even this did no good.

The following Christmas Eve she appeared as promptly as before, and frightened the guest in the room quite out of his senses by sitting down beside him, and gazing with her cavernous blue eyes into his. In her long, bony fingers bits of dripping seaweed were entwined, the ends hanging down, and these ends she drew across his forehead until he fainted away. He was found unconscious in his bed the next morning, simply saturated with sea-water and fright.

The next year the master of Harrowby Hall decided not to have the best spare bedroom opened at all, but the ghost appeared as usual in the room —that is, it was supposed she did, for the hangings were dripping wet the next morning. Finding no one there, she immediately set out to haunt the owner of Harrowby himself. She found him in his own cosy room, congratulating himself upon having outwitted her.

All of a sudden the curl went out of his hair, and he was as wet as if he had fallen into a rain barrel. When he saw before him the lady of the cavernous eyes and seaweed fingers he too fainted, but immediately came to, because the vast amount of water in his hair, trickling down over his face, revived him.

Now it so happened that the master of Harrowby was a brave man. He intended to find out a few things he felt he had a right to know. He would have liked to put on a dry suit of clothes first, but the ghost refused to leave him for an instant until her hour was up. In an effort to warm himself up he turned to the fire; it was an unfortunate move, because it brought the ghost directly over the fire, which immediately was extinguished.

At this he turned angrily to her, and said: "Far be it from me to be impolite to a woman, madam, but I wish you'd stop your infernal visits to this house. Go sit out on the lake, if you like that sort of thing; soak the rain barrel, if you wish; but do not come into a gentleman's house and soak him and his possessions in this way, I beg of you!"

"Henry Hartwick Oglethorpe," said the ghost, in a gurgling voice, "you don't know what you are talking about. You do not know that I am compelled to haunt this place year after year by my terrible fate. It is no pleasure for me to enter this house, and ruin everything I touch. I never aspired to be a shower bath, but it is my doom. Do you know who I am?"

"No, I don't," returned the master of Harrowby. "I should say you were the Lady of the Lake!"

"No, I am the Water Ghost of Harrowby Hall,

and I have held this highly unpleasant office for two hundred years tonight."

"How the deuce did you ever come to get elected?" asked the master.

"Through a mistake," replied the specter. "I am the ghost of that fair maiden whose picture hangs over the mantelpiece in the drawing-room."

"But what made you get this house into such a spot?"

"I was not to blame, sir," returned the lady. "It was my father's fault. He built Harrowby Hall, and the room I haunt was to have been mine. My father had it furnished in pink and yellow, knowing well that blue and gray was the only combination of colors I could bear. He did it to spite me, and I refused to live in the room. Then my father said that I could live there or on the lawn, he didn't care which. That night I ran from the house and jumped over the cliff into the sea."

"That was foolish," said the master of Harrowby.

"So I've heard," returned the ghost, "but I really never realized what I was doing until after I was drowned. I had been drowned a week when a sea nymph came to me. She informed me that I was to be one of her followers, and that my doom was to haunt Harrowby Hall for one hour every Christmas Eve throughout the rest of eternity. I was to haunt that room on such Christmas Eves as I found it occupied; and if it should turn out *not* to be occupied, I was to spend that hour with the head of the house."

"I'll sell the place."

"That you cannot do, for then I must appear to any purchaser, and reveal to him the awful secret of the house."

"Do you mean to tell me that on every Christmas Eve that I don't happen to have somebody in that guest-chamber, you are going to haunt me wherever I may be, taking all the curl out of my hair, putting out my fire, and soaking me through to the skin?" demanded the master.

"Yes, Oglethorpe. And what is more," said the water ghost, "it doesn't make the slightest difference where you are. If I find that room empty, wherever you may be I shall douse you with my spectral pres—"

Here the clock struck one, and immediately the ghost faded away. It was perhaps more a trickle

than a fading, but as a disappearance it was complete.

"By St. George and his Dragon!" cried the master of Harrowby, "I swear that next Christmas there'll be someone in the spare room, or I spend the night in a bathtub."

But when Christmas Eve came again the master of Harrowby was in his grave. He never recovered from the cold he caught that awful night. Harrowby Hall was closed, and the heir to the estate was in London. And there to him in his apartment came the water ghost at the appointed hour. Being younger and stronger, however, he survived the shock. Everything in his rooms was ruined—his clocks were rusted; a fine collection of watercolor drawings was entirely washed out. And because the apartments below his were drenched with water soaking through the floors, he was asked by his landlady to leave the apartment immediately.

The story of his family's ghost had gone about; no one would invite him to any party except afternoon teas and receptions, and fathers of daughters refused to allow him to remain in their houses later than eight o'clock at night.

So the heir of Harrowby Hall determined that something must be done.

The thought came to him to have the fireplace in the room enlarged, so that the ghost would evaporate at its first appearance. But he remembered his father's experience with the fire. Then he thought of steampipes. These, he remembered, could lie hundreds of feet deep in water, and still be hot enough to drive the water away in vapor. So the haunted room was heated by steam to a withering degree.

The scheme was only partially successful. The water ghost appeared at the specified time, but hot as the room was, it shortened her visit by no more than five minutes in the hour. And during this time the young master was a nervous wreck, and the room itself was terribly cracked and warped. And worse than this, as the last drop of the water ghost was slowly sizzling itself out on the floor, she whispered that there was still plenty of water where she came from, and that next year would find her as exasperatingly saturating as ever.

It was then that, going from one extreme to the other, the heir of Harrowby hit upon the means by which the water ghost was ultimately conquered, and happiness came once more to the house of Oglethorpe.

The heir provided himself with a warm suit of fur underclothing. Wearing this with the furry side in, he placed over it a tight-fitting rubber garment like a jersey. On top of this he drew on another set of woolen underclothing, and over this was a second rubber garment like the first. Upon his head he wore a light and comfortable diving helmet; and so clad, on the following Christmas Eve he awaited the coming of his tormentor.

It was a bitterly cold night that brought to a close this twenty-fourth day of December. The air outside was still, but the temperature was below zero. Within all was quiet; the servants of Harrowby Hall awaited with beating hearts the outcome of their master's campaign against his supernatural visitor.

The master himself was lying on the bed in the haunted room, dressed as he had planned and then . . .

The clock clanged out the hour of twelve.

There was a sudden banging of doors. A blast of cold air swept through the halls. The door leading into the haunted chamber flew open, a splash was heard, and the water ghost was seen standing at the side of the heir of Harrowby. Immediately from his clothing there streamed rivulets of water, but deep down under the various garments he wore he was as dry and warm as he could have wished.

"Ha!" said the young master of Harrowby. "I'm glad to see you."

"You are the most original man I've met, if that is true," returned the ghost. "May I ask where did you get that hat?"

"Certainly, madam," returned the master, courteously. "It is a little portable observatory I had made for just such emergencies as this. But tell me, is it true that you are doomed to follow me about for one mortal hour—to stand where I stand, to sit where I sit?"

"That is my happy fate," returned the lady.

"We'll go out on the lake," said the master, starting up.

"You can't get rid of me that way," returned the

113

ghost. "The water won't swallow me up; in fact, it will just add to my present bulk."

"Nevertheless," said the master, firmly, "we will go out on the lake."

"But my dear sir," returned the ghost, "it is fearfully cold out there. You will be frozen hard before you've been out ten minutes."

"Oh, no, I'll not," replied the master. "I am very warmly dressed. Come!" This last in a tone of command that made the ghost ripple.

And they started.

They had not gone far before the water ghost showed signs of distress.

"You walk too slowly," she said. "I am nearly frozen. I beg you, hurry!"

"I should like to oblige a lady," returned the master courteously, "but my clothes are rather heavy, and a hundred yards an hour is about my speed. Indeed, I think we had better sit down here on this snowdrift, and talk matters over."

"Do not! Do not do so, I beg!" cried the ghost. "Let us move on. I feel myself growing rigid as it is. If we stop here, I shall be frozen stiff."

"That, madam," said the master slowly, seating

himself on an ice cake—"that is why I have brought you here. We have been on this spot just ten minutes; we have fifty more. Take your time about it, madam, but freeze. That is all I ask of you."

"I cannot move my right leg now," cried the ghost, in despair, "and my overskirt is a solid sheet of ice. Oh, good, kind Mr. Oglethorpe, light a fire, and let me go free from these icy fetters."

"Never, madam. It cannot be. I have you at last."

"Alas!" cried the ghost, a tear trickling down her frozen cheek. "Help me, I beg. I congeal!"

"Congeal, madam, congeal!" returned Oglethorpe coldly. "You have drenched me and mine for two hundred and three years, madam. Tonight, you have had your last drench."

"Ah, but I shall thaw out again, and then you'll see. Instead of the comfortably warm, genial ghost I have been in the past, sir, I shall be ice water," cried the lady, threateningly.

"No, you won't either," returned Oglethorpe; "for when you are frozen quite stiff, I shall send you to a cold-storage warehouse, and there shall you remain an icy work of art forever more."

"But warehouses burn."

"So they do, but this warehouse cannot burn. It is made of asbestos and surrounding it are fire-proof walls, and within those walls the temperature is now and shall forever be 416 degrees below the zero point; low enough to make an icicle of any flame in this world—or the next," the master added, with a chuckle.

"For the last time I beseech you. I would go on my knees to you, Oglethorpe, if they were not already frozen. I beg of you do not doo—"

Here even the words froze on the water ghost's lips and the clock struck one. There was a momentary tremor throughout the icebound form, and the moon, coming out from behind a cloud, shone down on the rigid figure of a beautiful woman sculptured in clear, transparent ice. There stood the ghost of Harrowby Hall, conquered by the cold, a prisoner for all time.

The heir of Harrowby had won at last, and to-day in a large storage house in London stands the frigid form of one who will never again flood the house of Oglethorpe with woe and sea-water.